Money
Then and Now

Diana Noonan

Contents

Money

What Is Money?

When most people think of money, they think of notes and coins. But money can be anything that people are happy to **exchange** for something else. This makes money **valuable** and useful. Money is so valuable and useful that it would be almost impossible to live without it.

Different notes and coins are used in different countries around the world.

When people do work that other people think is valuable, they earn money. A hospital values a nurse's work, so the nurse is paid money for caring for patients. Pet owners value the work of a vet, so they pay the vet money for looking after the health of their pets.

Vets are paid to care for animals that are sick or injured.

Money can also be given as a gift to a friend or family member. For example, in some cultures, gifts of money are thrown towards the bride and groom as they perform a special dance at their wedding.

Money is useful because it can be exchanged for **goods** that people *need*. These goods include food, clothes, shelter and medicine. Money can also be exchanged for goods that people *want*. These include toys, electronic devices and jewellery.

People can choose to spend money on things that make their lives enjoyable, such as video games.

Money is also useful because it can be exchanged for **services**. These include the services people need in order to take care of themselves and the things they own, such as visits to the doctor and dentist, or repairs to people's homes. Money can also be exchanged for services that people want so they can enjoy life more. These can include a tour of a wildlife park, dinner at a restaurant or a flight to visit friends or family.

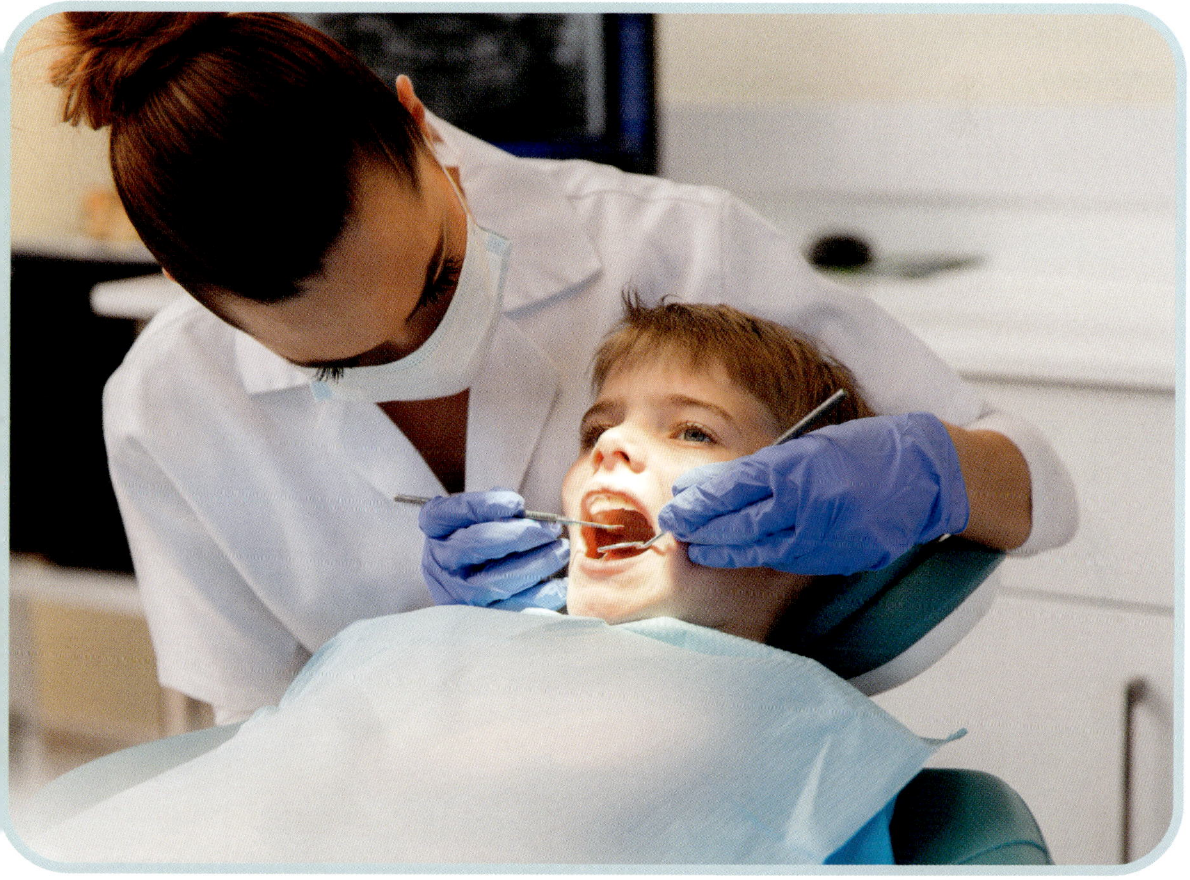

Dentists provide a service people need to have good dental health.

The History of Money

Before coins and notes were invented, people had to have something valuable to exchange for the goods and services they wanted. Throughout history, different kinds of valuable things have been exchanged.

Bartering

Bartering is the simplest and oldest form of exchange.

When people bartered, they exchanged their own goods or services for someone else's goods or services. The goods or services that were bartered were thought to be of similar value. This meant the barter felt like a fair deal to everyone involved.

> Examples of bartering included a farmer exchanging milk from their cow for bread from a baker, or a gardener exchanging vegetables from their garden for work from a builder.

This historical drawing shows European traders bartering.

In Papua New Guinea, the Motu people live in an area that is too dry to grow a crop they need called **sago**. However, their land has clay that is good for making cooking pots. For hundreds of years, the Motu people bartered some of their clay pots for sago grown by farmers in another part of Papua New Guinea.

The Motu men travelled long distances by sailing boat to exchange their clay pots. The journey home was slow and dangerous because the sago was so heavy. The Motu sailors' families were relieved when they finally arrived home with their valuable goods.

Motu men from Papua New Guinea used sailing boats and canoes on their trade journeys.

Tokens

While bartering was a successful form of exchange, it did have some problems. For example, it only worked if a person could find someone who had goods and services that they wanted, and who in turn wanted the goods and services that they had. It also only worked if the exchange felt like a fair deal for everyone. This wasn't always possible, which is why **tokens** became important.

Tokens have been used in trade for thousands of years. At first, they were rare and valuable items that could be exchanged for goods or services. They might be special shells and feathers, beads, whales' teeth or metal rings.

Thousands of years ago, tokens such as these shells were exchanged for goods or services.

Tokens worked well as a way of paying for goods and services, but there were problems with them, too. Some tokens, such as shells, broke easily or wore out too quickly. Other tokens, such as coloured feathers, were rare and valuable in one country, but not in another, where they were plentiful.

To make things simpler, people decided to make tokens specifically for exchanging. They called these tokens "money".

This 2000-year-old silver coin from ancient Rome had a different design on each side.

Coins and Notes

When countries made coins and printed notes, they followed special rules. Money had to be strong so it wouldn't break or wear out. It had to be easy to carry, and it had to come in different values. Most importantly, everyone had to agree that money was valuable.

The First Coins

Coins were the first money to be made. They were used around 600 **BCE** in the kingdom of Lydia, which is now part of Turkey. The Lydians followed all the rules: their coins were made of strong metal, and they were small, flat and easy to carry. Everyone knew they were valuable because they were made of a mixture of gold and silver.

One side of this ancient Lydian coin shows a lion and a bull, and the other side has two indented squares.

As news spread about coins and how useful they were, more countries started making their own. In some countries, coins were decorated with beautiful designs; in others, they were decorated with the faces of their leaders. In China, some coins were made with holes through them so they could be threaded on a string. This made them even easier to carry.

Some dishonest people tried to shave the valuable metal from coins. This was called "coin clipping".

Most ancient Chinese coins had a square hole in the middle.

Coins were very useful, but they also led to a big problem. As soon as someone had a lot of coins, the load became too heavy to carry. This was a serious problem for traders.

Traders were people who travelled around, buying goods from people in one place and selling them for a **profit** to people in another place. It didn't take long for traders to collect so many coins that it became difficult to carry them all at once.

This stone carving from ancient Greece shows a bread seller trading his goods.

Agents' Notes

Over two thousand years ago, Chinese traders were the first people to solve the problem of travelling with heavy coins. When a trader had too many coins to carry, they took them to a person they trusted. This person was called an "agent".

The agent agreed to keep the coins in a safe place and in return gave the trader a note written on leather. This note was proof that the money had been left with the agent. Agents' notes were easy to carry because they were light and could be folded up. The trader could use the note to buy goods. It was a way of telling the person who was selling the goods that the trader had enough coins to pay them at another time.

Large numbers of ancient Chinese coins were threaded with string and traded for an agent's note.

Printed Notes

Some Chinese agents began printing their notes on paper about 1200 years ago. The notes were printed with designs that were very difficult to copy so that criminals would not be able to make their own illegal notes. People who received this new printed "paper money" as payment for goods or services could take it to the place where it was made and exchange it for coins.

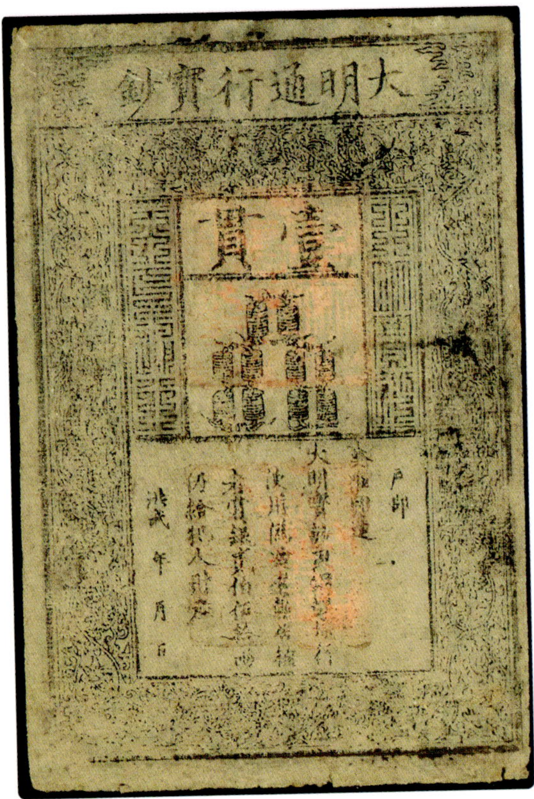

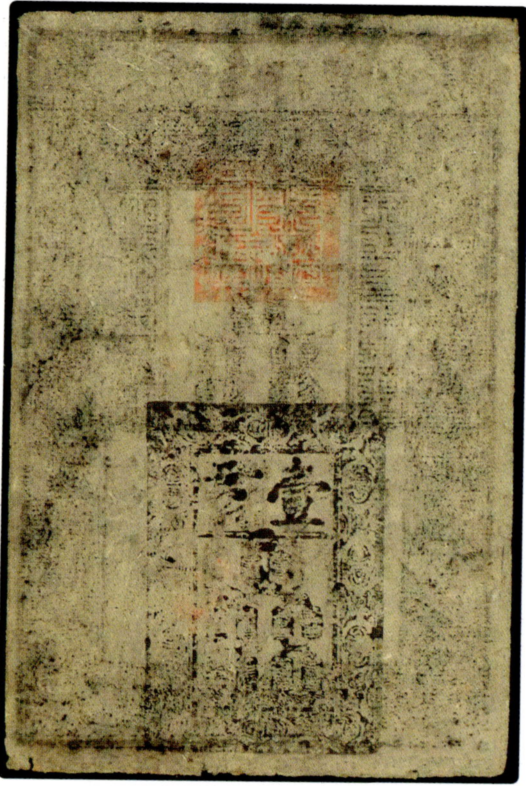

This early Chinese paper money was printed on special paper and featured a detailed design.

Countries around the world still make **currency** by printing notes and making coins. However, today's notes are made of a special soft plastic, and modern coins are not usually made of valuable metal.

Currency is still decorated with detailed designs that are difficult to copy. Some people like to collect currencies from around the world.

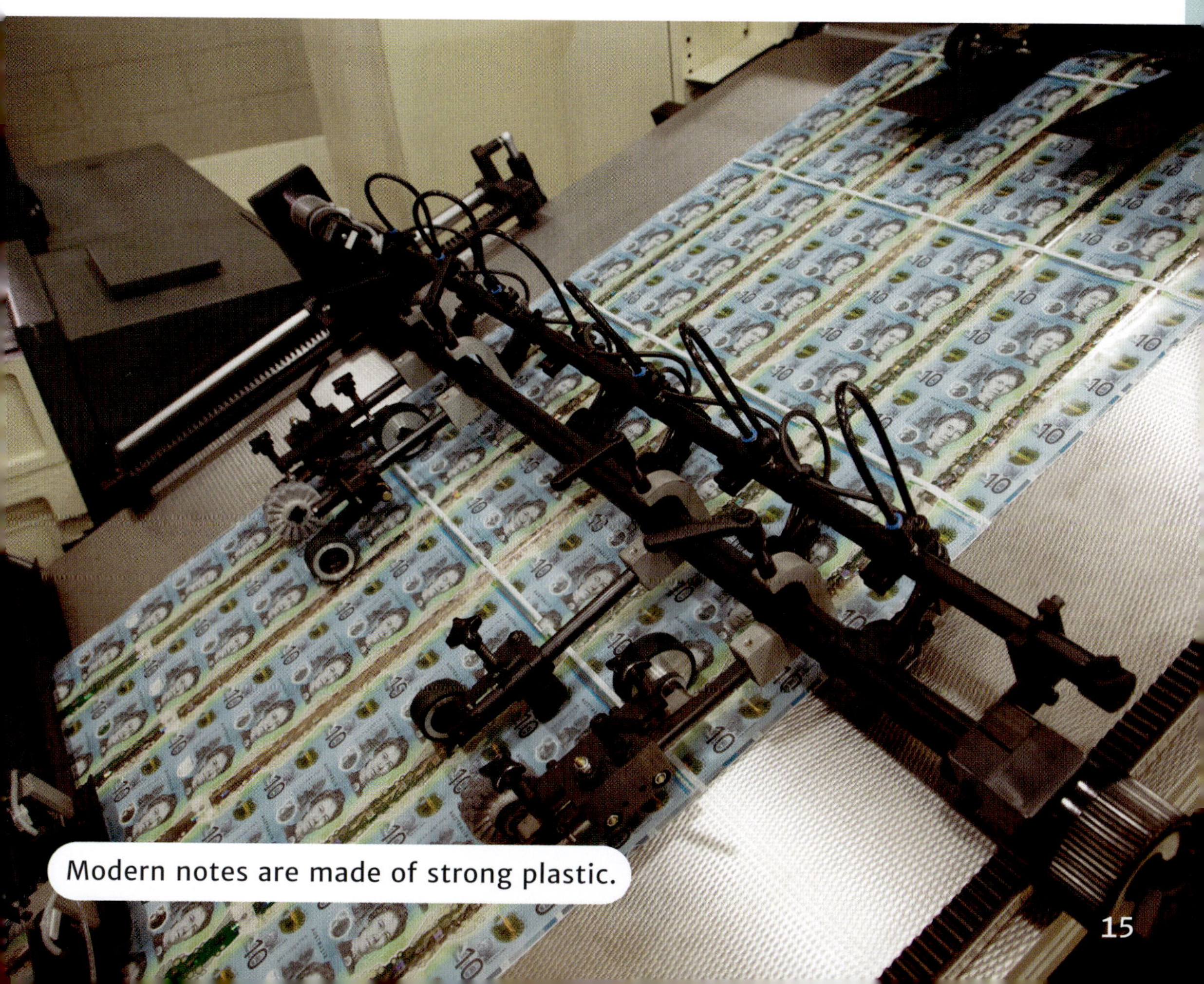

Modern notes are made of strong plastic.

Banks

A bank is a business that keeps money and valuables safe, and lends and borrows money. The people who own banks are called bankers.

In ancient Greece, banks helped traders from other countries by exchanging their coins for Greek coins. This meant the traders could then buy Greek goods. Banks in ancient Rome collected **taxes** for the government. Today, banks help people in many ways.

This bank in Siena, Italy, opened in 1472 and is the world's oldest operating bank.

Depositing Money

Some people like to carry a few coins and notes in their wallet or pocket. Carrying a lot of money isn't a good idea because it can get lost or stolen. People can go to a bank to set up a **bank account.** A bank is a safe place to **deposit** money when it's not being used.

Inside the bank, money is kept in a special room called a vault. This room has very thick walls that are made of extra-strong concrete. Security cameras and alarms help protect the vault from robberies.

People deposit items of value other than money at banks. These include jewellery, gold and important documents. They are stored in the bank's vault.

Bank vault doors are usually round and fitted with more than one lock.

Withdrawing Money

When a customer wants to use some of their money to pay for goods or services, or to give as a gift, they **withdraw** it from the bank. They can usually do this whenever they want. However, if they want to withdraw a very large amount they need to tell the bank ahead of time. Until a customer withdraws their money, the bank uses it to help other customers, such as those who want to borrow money.

Banks usually charge customers a fee for looking after their money and valuable items.

Customers can visit a bank to withdraw money from their account.

Borrowing Money

People sometimes do not have enough money to buy the goods or services they want. This is especially true if they want to buy an expensive item such as a house or a car.

Banks can help by lending people money. After an agreed time, the borrowed money is paid back to the bank. Banks charge a fee for customers to borrow money.

People often need to borrow money from a bank to buy an expensive item such as a car.

Money and the Internet

Today, there are many ways to pay and be paid for goods and services. These include **cash**, bank cards and online banking. What has helped the most is the internet.

The internet is a way of linking together millions of computers and devices from all around the world. It means that banks and their customers can very quickly pass on banking information to each other.

A teenager uses online banking to buy something on her laptop.

Debit Cards

A debit card is a small plastic card that a bank can give to its customers. It is easy to carry and use. The debit card can be scanned electronically to instantly connect to a person's bank account and withdraw or transfer money from it.

The first debit cards were used in 1967 by a bank in London, England.

Each debit card has a PIN (personal identification number) to keep it safe. Only someone who knows the PIN can use the card.

A customer pays for groceries using a debit card.

Credit Cards

A credit card is a special kind of bank card. It can be used like a debit card to buy goods and services without cash. When people use a credit card, they are borrowing money from the bank, rather than taking it from their savings. The money must be paid back to the bank after an agreed time. The bank charges the customer to use a credit card.

People often use a credit card to pay for expensive items such as televisions.

ATMs

Automated teller machines **(ATMs)** are like mini banks. They can be found in cities, towns and suburbs around the world. Customers can use their debit or credit cards at ATMs to find out information about their bank accounts. They can also use ATMs to withdraw notes from their account and deposit notes into them.

A man uses his bank card at an ATM.

This ATM is in Chiang Mai, Thailand.

Online Banking

Many people with internet access do their banking online. This means they use a computer or a device to pay for goods and services, and to check how much money they have in their bank account.

A woman in a remote village in Thailand uses a laptop to do her banking online.

Some people use the internet to send a special type of digital money anywhere in the world, without using a bank. This money is called "cryptocurrency". It can be used to buy and sell goods and services.

Everyone who uses cryptocurrency keeps online records of their own and everyone else's buying and selling activity (or they pay someone to do this for them). Cryptocurrency feels safe and fair because everyone can see everyone else's activity!

One problem with cryptocurrencies is that the computers that manage them need a lot of electricity. And making electricity isn't always good for the environment.

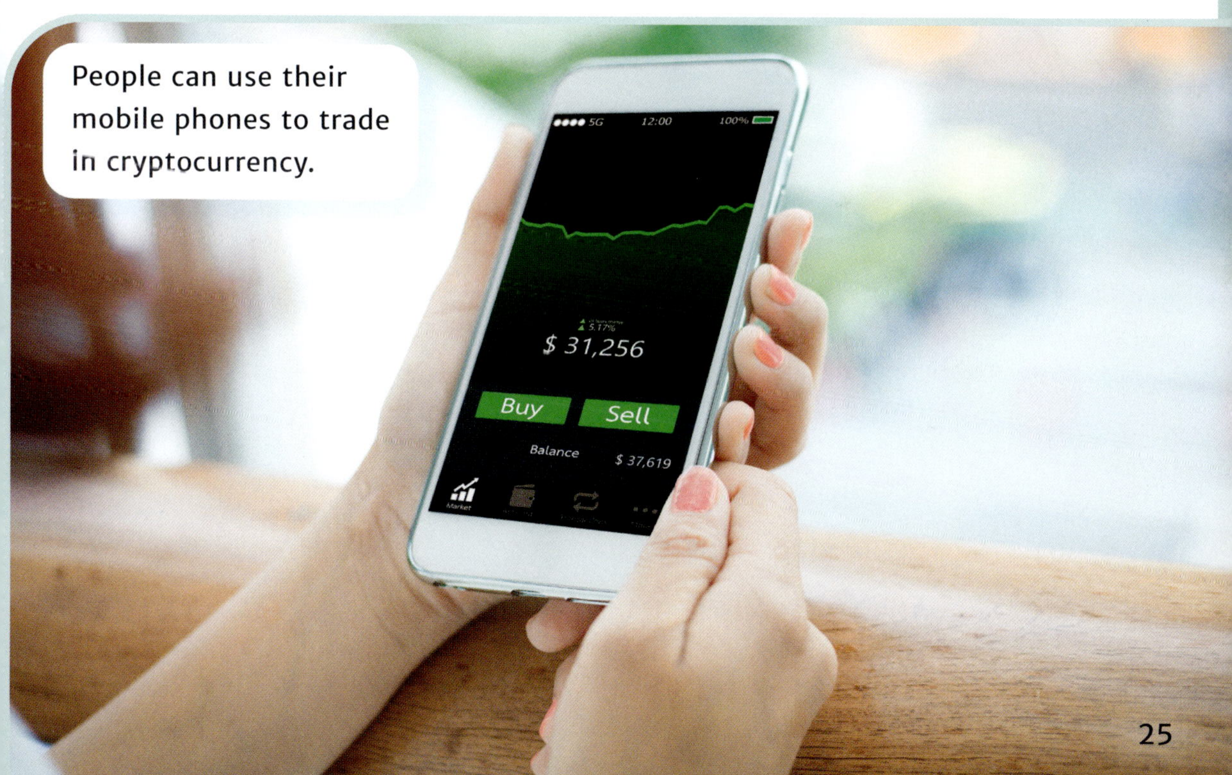

People can use their mobile phones to trade in cryptocurrency.

From bartering to banking, the ways in which people pay for the things they need and want have changed greatly over the centuries. They are still changing today as people continue to invent new ways to pay and be paid for goods and services. What will never change is that goods and services are valuable, and people must always have some kind of money to pay for them.

A woman uses her phone to pay for her goods.

My Super Savings Plan

By Sefa Smith

Last Friday afternoon, at the mall, I saw some colourful headphones. They were on sale for $35 – but only for one more week. The next Friday, they would cost $70. I wished I could buy the headphones while they were on sale, but I had only $5 in my bank account.

If I wanted the headphones while they were still half price, I had to find some ways to make money – and fast!

That night, I thought of a plan. First, I made a graph to help me keep track of my money. I called it "Sefa's Super Savings Plan".

Next, I asked Mum if she had any jobs that I could do to earn money. Mum said she would pay me $5 next Friday if I swept the path every day for a week. I said I would.

On Saturday morning, I swept the path for the first time and made sure Mum saw me doing it!

On Saturday night, Dad used his online banking app to deposit my weekly $5 pocket money into my account. The line on my savings graph showed I now had $10 in my bank account!

Next, I asked my brother, Lucas, if he would pay me to wash his car on Tuesday after he got home from work. He agreed, and on Tuesday night he deposited $10 into my bank account.

I updated my graph, which now showed I had $20 in the bank – but Friday was getting closer, and even with the $5 Mum was going to pay me for sweeping the path, I still wouldn't have all the money I needed for the headphones.

Then, I got a big surprise! Grandma phoned on Wednesday night. She'd heard I was looking for jobs, and she said she would pay me $10 to be her golf **caddie** on Friday after school. I couldn't wait! I looked at my graph in amazement. With Grandma's $10, I would have enough money for the headphones!

On Friday morning, Mum paid me my $5 for sweeping the path.

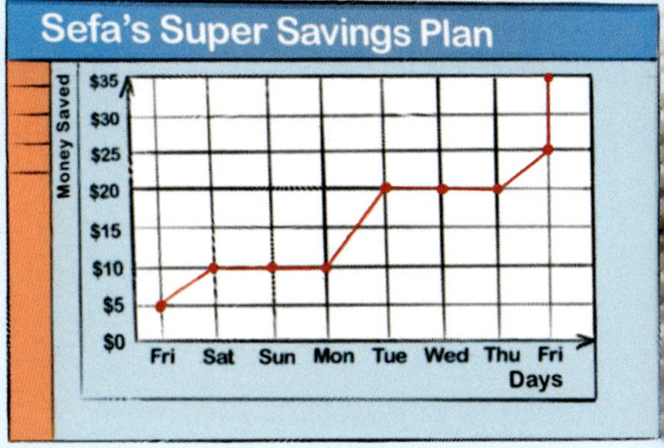

After school, I rode my bike to the golf course to meet Grandma and caddied for her for three hours. Afterwards, I put the $10 she gave me into my pocket. I hurried home because the mall was closing in one hour, and Dad was taking me to buy the headphones!

However, when I arrived home, I couldn't find Grandma's $10 note anywhere. It must have fallen out of my pocket as I was riding my bike!

Dad drove me back along the road to search for the $10, but we couldn't find it anywhere. I almost felt like crying, because the sale would be over before I had enough money to pay for the headphones.

Then, I had an idea. I asked Dad if he would pay me $10 in advance if I took our dog, Jasper, to the dog park for him, every night for a week.

Dad replied that he would, and away we went to the mall. Dad used his banking app to transfer my savings to his account, then he used his debit card to pay for the headphones.

That evening, I took Jasper to the dog park. I couldn't hear him barking at all the other dogs – because I was listening to music on my new headphones!

Glossary

ATMs (*noun*) machines that let people add money to or take money from their bank accounts

bank account (*noun*) a record kept by a bank that shows how much money a customer has

BCE (*adjective*) Before the Common Era, the time dates are counted from

caddie (*noun*) a person who helps a golfer by carrying their equipment

cash (*noun*) coins and notes

currency (*noun*) a system of money used in a particular country

deposit (*verb*) to put money in a bank account

exchange (*verb*) to give something and receive something in return

goods (*noun*) items that are bought and sold

profit (*noun*) the difference between what is paid for something and the amount it is sold for

sago (*noun*) a thick substance, made from palm trees, that is used in many foods

services (*noun*) tasks that are done for a customer

taxes (*noun*) — money paid to the government by people and businesses

tokens (*noun*) — items used instead of money

valuable (*adjective*) — worth something

withdraw (*verb*) — to take money out of a bank account

Index